Blame it on the Big Blue Panda!

To Mavis and all the lovely staff at Leigh Library

C.F.

For Mum and Chris

T.D.

For my parents

E.C.

This edition published by Parragon Books Ltd in 2013 and distributed by

Parragon Inc.
440 Park Avenue South, 13th Floor
New York, NY 10016
www.parragon.com

Published by arrangement with Gullane Children's Books
Text: © Claire Freedman 2006
Illustrations: © Emma Carlow and Trevor Dickinson 2006

ISBN 978-1-4723-3186-1

Printed in China

Blame it on the Big Blue Panda!

Claire Freedman

illustrated by **Emma Carlow & Trevor Dickinson**

Parragon

Bath · New York · Cologne · Melbourne · Delhi
Hong Kong · Shenzhen · Singapore · Amsterdam

Mrs. Panda loved her little Pandy so much. But he was so naughty and told the most terrible fibs! "Don't climb any tall trees!" Mrs. Panda said, when Pandy went outside, playing. "Not without me there!" "I won't!" Pandy promised.

But when Mrs. Panda called Pandy in for lunch, she found him clinging to the top branches of the highest tree ever!

"Pandy, what did I tell you about climbing so high?" Mrs. Panda said, sternly. "Come down before you fall!"

"It wasn't me!" Pandy cried.
"It was the **Big Blue Panda . . . .**

He jumped from the
bushes, grabbed me, and
carried me up here!"
"Really?" said his mom.
"So where is this
Big Blue Panda now?"

"He ran away," Pandy replied.
"That's why you didn't see him!"

That week, Pandy and his mom went shopping at the supermarket. "Don't run off," Mrs. Panda said. "And please don't touch anything!"

Pandy's mom turned around to get a shopping cart.
When she looked around again, Pandy had vanished . . . .

Then she spotted him—lying on
a huge pile of squashed cereal boxes!
"Oh, Pandy!" Mrs. Panda cried. "You are naughty!"

"It wasn't me!" said Pandy.

"It was the **Big Blue Panda!**
He whizzed down the aisle on
roller skates, scooped me up, and
threw me onto these boxes before
I could stop him!"

"And I suppose no one
saw him but you?"

Mrs. Panda glared.

"Yes!" Pandy nodded.
"The **Big Blue Panda** is
faster than lightning!"

Days later, Mrs. Panda baked one of her yummy chocolate fudge cakes. While she cleaned up, she left the cake in the dining room. That was where Pandy was found, surrounded by cake crumbs, with chocolate frosting all over his mouth!

"Pandy, you greedy bear!"
his mom cried.
"I didn't eat it!"
mumbled Pandy,
wiping sticky paws
on the tablecloth . . . .

"The **Big Blue Panda** swung in through the window and snatched the cake! He gobbled it up before I could shout for help!"

Mrs. Panda stared at Pandy with an
angry look.
"We both know there is
no such thing as the
Big Blue Panda,
and it's YOU who's been naughty,"
she said.

"It WAS the **Big Blue Panda**,"
Pandy insisted.

"Then maybe I had better
DO something about him,"
sighed Mom.

Two days later, a letter
arrived in the mail for Pandy.
"Who could it be from?" Pandy cried,
excitedly. He ripped open the
envelope and read . . .

Dear Pandy,

I am very upset to hear
you have been blaming ME
for all your bad behavior.
I am going to come and talk
to you this friday afternoon!
Be there!

from

The Big Blue

Panda

Main street
USA

Pandy dropped his breakfast in his lap with shock!
"Oh dear," his mom said. "The **Big Blue Panda**
doesn't seem very happy with you!"
"B-b-but I only pretended there was a **Big Blue Panda**!"
gasped Pandy. "He doesn't really exist—does he?"
"Maybe he does!" Mom replied, trying to hide her smile.

Pandy was very worried.
**"Friday is only three days from
now!"**
he cried.
"What am I going to do?"

"I think you should try
to be very, very good!"
his mom advised.
"You don't want to upset
the **Big Blue Panda**
any further!"

So Pandy was on his best behavior. He stopped taking cookies from the jar when Mrs. Panda's back was turned.

He had his bath every night, with only a teeny bit of complaining.
And he didn't tell one single fib.

Then, on Friday morning, the mailman brought a second letter.

Main street
USA

Dear Pandy,

I hear you have been behaving yourself since I wrote. I'm glad to say there is no need for me to visit you after all.

from

The Big Blue Panda

P.S. Tomorrow I am going exploring down the Wigga-Wagga River and will be away for 5 years!

Pandy breathed out a huge sigh of relief. "Hurray! The **Big Blue Panda** isn't coming after all!" he told his mom. "What a lucky escape!" Mrs. Panda said, with a twinkle in her eye.

"I'll never blame anything on
the Big Blue Panda ever again!"
Pandy promised. "From now on,
I will be really good!"
"I'm happy to hear it!"
grinned his mom.

And Pandy was good (for him!) . . .
almost all of the time!